Garbage In, Gospel Out

or
Do You Like the View?

Garbage In, Gospel Out

or
Do You Like the View?

"Incorrect or poor quality input will
always produce faulty output."

Jean-Paul L. Garnier

SPACE COWBOY BOOKS

SPACE COWBOY BOOKS
61871 Twentynine Palms Hwy
Joshua Tree, CA 92252
www.spacecowboybooks.com

Garbage In, Gospel Out
ISBN #978-1-7328257-2-7

First Edition | 2020
Cover Art by Zara Kand

This book is dedicated to corporate America
and its attitude of short term gain
in exchange for long term tragedy.

Frank removed himself from subjective reality. He rubbed salt on his teeth before entering an artificial tropical storm. Basking in the warm rain he smeared his entire body with pig fat. He wiped the water and fat from his limbs and torso with spent seed casings, then hid his nudity with animal hair. From the bedroom he moved to the kitchen, where he ate several reproductive organs. He went outside and lit an ancient forest on fire. The forest burned in a series of explosions until he put the fire out in front of a huge pile of powdered stone. Pushing a button he added an arbitrary measurement to a handful of flattened dead plants. After preserving the measurement he moved on to exchanging various items for a symbol of an idea. He enjoyed the symbol, or rather the idea, and it was this very idea that had dragged him from his rectangle of coiled metal as a ball of fire floated above the edge of the Earth.

Reports and the Bureau

After only several weeks working for the Bureau Frank had already fallen behind on the work. His employer's demand for falsity and speed outmatched any he had encountered before. But he was a good reporter, or rather falsifier of reports, and had earned this position fair and square. He knew he could catch up, perhaps if things at home were going better...

On the clock. The reports needed to be disseminated quickly and accurately. Although Frank never knew which report was headed where, he didn't mind, despite the stress he enjoyed the job. In fact, he had been somewhat lucky to get the job, other qualified reporters had applied alongside him, but the superiors assured him that he had a special quality they desired. They had called this quality: unrestrained flightiness with an obsessive detail fixation. The description had made him uncomfortable but he shrugged it off. Work was work.

On the clock. Time to report.

The Foundation room is an exclusive, world famous, house of additional regulatory programs. Members are able to choose different days of activation. Members enjoy: advance notice, complimentary customers, and additional upscale personal service. Membership dues support U.S. roaming partners.

The International Foundation for Information calls this network "an infinitely subtle confrontation of directly independent suppliers". Accessor-

ies may substitute their work, or may transfer their qualifying rate plans, after the debate is processed. Allow an instrumental and willing trust: On Our Terms and Conditions. Courage and patience yields several firming agents, resulting in improved career. This may require inhibited degradation – what the work is.   Media enzymes contribute to the firming agents of an unwritten deathbed, a performance that lasts days and nights.

Frank looked up from his report to see his superior silently looming over him. The ambiguous man had a grey look about him, but overall appeared superficially happy and pleased. Frank didn't like to work with someone at his shoulder, but the Bureau always stood behind shoulders, looking over and past what a man did – all the way through to his deep hidden desires.   This grey Manager barely stirred and said nothing, giving Frank the unease of painted statue performers in crumby tourist areas. Finally the man spoke.

"We hope you are as pleased as we are with your progress. Your reports have the deep accuracy that we were looking for, very convincing, to say the least. Frank, you are a fine addition to our team. Your wife must be terribly proud of you."

Frank didn't like the way the man said *wife*. He knew they had run extensive background checks and probably knew everything there was to know about him. Still, he was always uncomfortable when another man mentioned Samantha. The comment seemed out of place.

"Thank you, Sir. I enjoy reporting. Duty to Citizen and Country, you know? As I was trained, it is not about the report itself, not about the man who writes them, but for the good of the world. I enjoy the selfless act of reporting. I enjoy your compliments and satisfaction with my work."

With a single utterance of "Good" his superior turned and left Frank to his work. A finely oiled machine. Pleasure had dripped from the man's words. He must have been an expert reporter in his time. The Bureau required that all employees enjoy their work. Some of the superiors had even been quoted saying, "Smiling Pays the Bills".

On the clock. Time to report.

If for any reason you are not completely satisfied apply for permits and disregard most of it. Out went the incredible guarantee, because everything we say is illegal black documents. Two agents were accused of murdering 100% money back guarantee. But we do not have playgrounds sur-

rounded with guardhouse atmosphere. The first penis enlargement pill got distracted. The research company is knee deep in the miscarriage of justice, plus the edit formations of defamed international business. You're handed a camera. You'll probably read somewhere that average eyes have thinner class. As for penis size, average subsequently. You've made movies, you're not satisfied. Signs of aging show up intense. You can take the damage. All know this.

Report filed with satisfaction. Fortunately Frank didn't have to lie about enjoying the work. He had, after all, greatly strived to achieve his position. Every report placed into the tubes that worked its way to the offices of the Managers filled him with a great sense of purpose, even if he would never be illuminated as to what that purpose was.

With equal satisfaction his car turned over easy. One stop on the way home, for his wife, then onto his own private pleasure. If Samantha was in a good mood, all the better. Tonight was the night that his favorite program aired. *History: Low and High Points*. He wasn't alone in his love for the show. In fact, it was so popular that some felt it had become obligatory to watch. Wednesday night ritual.

He pulled the car into the liquor store parking lot. Objects shining in the next door pawn shop window distracted him. A glittering silver ocean of treasures. Maybe a present for Samantha. Maybe it could soothe their row. Maybe… Maybe…

The Device

Frank shifted around in his pocket and thumbed at the small device. He'd been too scared to push the button, but he knew that he couldn't resist the temptation for much longer. Removing his hand from his pocket he switched the blinker on, signaling his intent to exit the freeway. The driver to his right sped up, blocking his passage, causing him to miss his exit. Glancing at the rearview his saw his face contort in grimace. His fingers found their way back to the device and without thinking he pushed the button. The blinker still flashed. He turned his head to the right and saw the line of cars back off to let him pass.

Off the freeway Frank noticed that all the cars were yielding to him. When he arrived at an intersection at the same time as another car the driver waved for him to go first. He'd forgotten to turn the device off. He almost pushed the button again, then refrained, deciding to wait until the drive was over. It was smooth sailing for the rest of the ride.

The pettiness switch really does make life a lot easier. Do I actually need to turn it off? He didn't say anything about leaving it on for long periods, he'd only said that the switch would turn off the pettiness of others. A strange pawn shop find. Frank had bought the device on impulse, thinking it would be a good gift for his wife, who was always complaining about how petty people can be. As he was turning the knob of the front door he experienced a moment of hesitation and hit the switch once more before entering the house.

Samantha, his wife, sat watching the soaps, barely noticing his entrance. He threw his keys into the dish with a loud clank. Only then did Samantha stir. Without looking up from the TV she asked, "Did you remember to stop and get me more Chablis?" He had not. The strangeness of finding the device and the courteous drive had made him forget all about her request.

Frank was about to leave the house again, for the forgotten errand, when he decided to push the button. His fingers hadn't left the device when he heard Samantha call out, "Don't worry about it, I'm sure you've had a long day, we still have some Chardonnay. Why don't you sit down and I'll pour us a glass."

He was shocked. She was never kind to him when he got home from work. Usually she just wanted to give him an earful of TV gossip and complaints. She was still talking to him, but he didn't hear. On the television a political debate was taking place, but the candidates were not debating. Instead, a series of apologies were taking place. The talking heads praised each other and spoke of each other's favorable qualities. *What could be going on, did the world change on my way home? Is this my doing?*

He thumbed the device once more. The politicians froze for a minute with shocked looks on their faces. As they returned to arguing his wife spilled wine all over the floor. "Damn it, Frank. I thought I asked you to pick up Chablis. You know I hate Chardonnay in the early evening."

He pushed the button again. "Oh, how clumsy I am." Samantha said to herself as she grabbed a towel and started cleaning up the mess. On the television the argument reverted to an almost sycophantic shower of compliments. Each candidate patiently waiting for the other to finish before rebutting with a comment equally polite.

Frank went into the front yard to clear his head. Passersby waved from car windows. He pushed the button again and watched their demeanors change. The waving stopped as people ignored him and went back to navigating the thick traffic. A hand extended from a car window and from the hand extended a middle finger. The driver shouted insults at a passing vehicle. Frank couldn't resist hitting the button again, and again the moods of the drivers changed. *This thing really works. Pettiness disappears instantly when I activate the device. I could do a lot of good for the world with this thing.* He shuddered at the power that rested in his palm. Quickly he shut it off, fearful of the awesome control he now had over others.

Walking back in the house he was greeted with more of Samantha's complaints. He sat on the couch trying to ignore the insult. The politicians were back to their mud-slinging. Samantha was already drunk. Her volume was rising in intensity. *I can do something about it, why shouldn't I?* The allure of the button tainted his judgement and he pushed it without further thought. Samantha settled down. Through his thoughts he even heard her utter a kind word.

His mood sank. *Why didn't the man at the pawn shop warn me? This device may turn off the pettiness of others, but every time I reach for the button I'm being petty myself...* Frank sat up from the couch and went outside once more. He hit the button one last time, turning the pettiness of the world back on, then lifted the lid of the trash can and chucked the device in with the rest of the rubbish.

The First Message

"As long as these lasers remain on, from this moment on, persons in the future can transmit information back to any point in the past since we turned the device on, as long as it continues to run. With these new super-cooled superconductors we should be able to keep the machine running for an indefinite amount of time, and at little cost. All systems running, let's give it a test. System on. Wow, it looks like we are receiving a message already. It's amazing someone chose the very moment we activated the machine."

"What does it say?"

"Turn the machine off."

Special Report

Frank arrived to work early and full of enthusiasm. He was inspired by so many programs, to be part of one himself crowned his life with a long term pasty smile. Samantha would grow to understand. She didn't like that he was forbidden to discuss his work. Yet this air of secrecy made him appear important. It was almost more satisfying not to talk about his job to her friends. Their curiosity inflated her. Gossip was always better when you couldn't quite place the sources.

Still smiling, Frank set up at his desk. He had been thinking about today's report. The thoughts brought him enjoyment. The enjoyment resulted in better reports. He would climb his way to the top on a ladder of words. He had a feeling about today's report.

On the clock. Time to report.

In this age of increasing, when we received the call about digital romance, I jumped at the chance of hearing the two old-fashioned words: anyone keeping. The Film: Kelly Metro is a flaming star absolutely alive! She's a buxom bombshell whom I have worshipped in the far away tradition of the still haul. In person she is bound to coax every rich tone and detail out of a scene. The talent is on schedule, running onto silver paper. The scams of the day give me a perfectly smooth tone. A great opportunity to chat with the Format Master. Oddly enough, we are first to experience the work of strippers. Who'd have guessed?

No studying with the masters. This is rocket science, folks. Learn the reason for the sexy story, ins and outs, sharp, clean and working. Shot on large negatives, becoming her ambition, she creates art out of the ephemera. Finally the girl of everyday life appears, out of a magazine advertisement, typically red. She shouts in silly western drawl, "Gone are the last details. Come on people, let's flood western consciousness with big tits, a naked renewed stream of images."

"Say, Butcher. For a while now I've been ready for the radioactivity series." He claims to have witnessed some serious fucking. Only fools attack his large scale negatives.

Exhibition art: A bird, rubbed with a salty paste. Cloves of you, forcing efforts. The influence was clear. Consider extra wide simmering compositions, the pieces presented. The board's selection has a disconcerting resemblance to the fans. Scenes of violent struggle, ink on paper, wrapped a couple of times around your waist, your digital exposure. Stretches of time following your completion of the next day. Hand pulling may be the most economical line of force.

As I walked I asked her why she'd open her skirt so it rose up so obviously. "Because under the table, it's about atomic war. Do you like the view?" She smiled while asking the survivors, "Will you envy the dead? Many warned."

"Let's talk about the space of everyday life, upstairs." Naturally eyes bulged in front of our pants. We both went upstairs and told them to get out.

The Manager stood like a hawk. Pleasure grimaced his rather weighty face. "It's my favorite so far. Your best work."

Frank wondered how the report had been read already. It hadn't even been printed and reduced yet. "Thank you, Sir. I am enjoying the work. The work is a real pleasure."

"Upstairs we see your value. A fine addition to the team. This report will please the brass in ways you cannot anticipate. In fact, you've caught their attention today. It's the reason for my visit. We have a more, um, personal task for you to complete. Your intrinsic value has been recognized. By the way, have we met before today? You face is familiar. Perhaps there are others like yours."

"I just try to blend in, Sir. I am pleased that the Managers are pleased. I'd be happy to take on any report that comes down the tubes. Really, I enjoy new assignments." Frank followed the statement with a shining smile.

"All very well. As I mentioned this report is of a more personal nature. We'd like you to go back as far as you can remember and report on your findings. This report is *above top secret* and should not be mentioned to the other Managers, or anyone for that matter. I will be your sole contact concerning this issue. No questions are to be asked. The report itself will guide you to the findings. I think you know what I mean."

Frank wasn't following him. The Managers could be cryptic at times, though they always made it clear if they were pleased or not. This request would be considered by most to be a promotion. "I think I follow you, Sir. At what time would you like the report started? I can begin right away and will take pleasure in doing so. I view the request as a compliment."

"Careful not to be too presumptuous. We expect the report by the end of the day. Remember – Smiling Pays the Bills."

So it wasn't a rumor. Frank smiled. Unsure what the Manager had meant by *a more personal nature*. When writing a report they always started off difficult then began to flow as the writing progressed. So he began.

Access Code

"Sir, please provide your simultaneous time access code."

"What are you talking about? I mean how is it that I am here now? It's as if my consciousness has split and I am in two places at once."

"That's all well and good, the way of things, really. But I will still be needing your simultaneous time access code, no one is allowed such access without one, as is common knowledge."

"Access code? Clearly I have just appeared here, you must have seen me appear out of nowhere."

"You speak as though these things are not common knowledge, what gives?"

Predictive Future

I'm so excited about the future. The fact that you have a great way to go back in time for me and my friends. It's so much better than just thinking about it. I don't know how much can be found the first time, since I've been trying for so many times, it can become difficult to remember. The only way to get the same time as the first, the first half, before it is the only thing that would have been, now is not alone, but hides waiting to be re-

membered. I love the new version, and I love the new update too. The new one is going to be the first. The first time since the beginning. The first place for the next few. I have to go back in time and it will be the same as the first time. When you get to see, you soon enough will recognize you have been in the first time. Since then it is not the only one of those days. When I get to see you in the first place I have to go back to the first time. The new problem of the day after, the only thing that would make it so much better now. I don't think that it was the only way. I'm at the end of the best thing ever, when you get a new one, for the next few days ago, when the first time is the first place. Time is a very long circle of the biggest challenge in the world. To all of them, to be able to see the same time as the first time. What the actual number of times I've had is the most recent version, and it is not the only way to get to the first time. Actually, it does not mean that you can get the same time twice, as many people have.

Once, I got to be the first. The new one for the rest of the last few. I have a great way to get to the first time. I love it when people say they will be the first, but it would have been in the first half, the first place, the first time. Since then I think it's time to go back to the point where he'll do it again, in a while. Travelers who want it all day long need some new friends. To be the first place in the first time. Times like this one are going to be the same time as the first. Only one who has been in the first time can tell the difference.

Sweat clung to Frank's brow. His feverish pace left a deep pit of hunger in his stomach. *The report is more personal. First Person*? What was it the Bureau had actually requested of him? Whatever it was it had poured out into his machine. *I hope the Managers are pleased.* He fit a smile to his face and waited expectedly for the return of his point of contact.

"Finished already are you?" The Manager stood grinning. He appeared as if he had never moved from his spot before or after the writing of the report. "We have big things in mind for you… If you keep up the good work. I'd like you to follow me upstairs for a debriefing. That is, when you are finished sending your report up the tubes. I'm sure you'd like to hand it over in person, but we're not going to let your victories interfere with protocol." His icy stature looked as if he were growing in place. Taller than before he smiled down at Frank. A smile that dripped accuracy.

Frank returned the smile and sent the report up the tube. The report rose and circled through the maze of piping. It joined others in a pile awaiting circulation at the editor's desk. The faceless editors worked harder than anyone else – the only barrier between the reporters and the brass.

The Manager led Frank into a small windowless office where the debriefing was to take place. "We're afraid that you might be too close to the project." said the man behind the desk. His dress lacked the formality of his position. His smile was genuine and threatening at the same time. "Has the stress of the job begun to overtake you? No shame in it, it happens to a lot of our new recruits."

"I thought you were pleased with the reports?" replied Frank.

"Oh, yes. We are. Quite pleased. Your last report on the other hand… It's your accuracy. You know at the Bureau we uphold a certain set of standards?"

"I am aware, Sir. My accuracy ratings are in the upwards of the 90 percentile. If I have deviated please know that it is not an indication of how much I am enjoying the work."

"We know where your loyalties lie. In fact, we have bigger reports that we would like you to take on. Think of it as a challenge. Not all of our new recruits are so lucky as to be handed such responsibility. Your report on time travel is pivotal. Surely you knew its potential to stir things up. We will need to question you further. You don't have clearance to discuss certain properties of your report. Yet, we asked. If you are showing a level of involvement that we were unaware of you will need to answer for it. Are you personally involved with any of the Managers?" Throughout the Manager's words his smile never ceased.

"No, Sir. I come and go as the others do. The tubes are my only connection with the upstairs. Just happy to be enjoying my work. I am also pleased at the faith the Bureau has placed in me. Of course, I will always answer any questions asked of me."

"Please wait here, Frank." The man behind the desk and the man that had led him to the office disappeared through a door in the back leaving Frank to sweat and wonder about what his transgression had been.

He was left sitting in the barren room for what felt like hours. There was nothing to occupy the time. Time acted as if it was at a standstill. Attempting to slow his heartbeat Frank began counting. At least it was something to occupy the time. When he reached 12,284 the man who had been sitting behind the desk returned.

"In light of your last report the Bureau requests that you work double shifts for the next few weeks. You seem, after all, to be able to occupy two spaces / times at once, this skill will help you with the task at hand. Consider it a promotion based on urgency. You will join the *Urgency Agency*. Instruction will not be necessary as you have shown your commitment to the indoctrination process. You will stay in the same office, but you will be limited to contact with a single liaison. At the end of each work day we will meet... To discuss your future."

The man led Frank out to the hallway and back to his office. Work was to begin immediately, but the nature of his reports wasn't stated. Sometimes ambiguity was the message. Back in his office, Frank stared at the wall uncertain of how to progress. He made sure to keep smiling during his moments of inactivity. He was unprepared for the additional workload. Three weeks into his new job he was already dreaming of time off. Perhaps if he was in a car crash on his way home they would have to give him medical leave. He could blame the incident on fatigue.

Back Injury

Sometimes his writhing was impossible to contain. The convulsions would erupt in wild unstoppable motions that had an ugly glare about them. When he got this way you had one of two choices: ride it out in hopes that you would remain unscathed, or put him down, usually the best way. Always seemed to work to pump him up full of something and let him go.

On one such episode the fit went to such extremes that his flailing could not be stopped, even with chemical intervention. The beast swung round the bed, ripping at everything, until it became so vulgar that his back arched up in horrid motion and a ghoulish crack was heard. This time he'd broken his own back, the fool. Everyone had been waiting for just such an event. Not in anyone's mind was it ever far off that something like this would happen.

In Arizona State, cripples are robbed three times as often as upright folks. It seems that such a cowardly act would be prevalent in other states as well, but it was to be more of an epidemic here for some reason. Because of this many of the less fortunate carried weapons and were becoming quite a force. At times robberies would go sour and there'd be blood on the wheelchair.

They started gangs and began getting into a little crime and robbing of their own. The upright found themselves at a standstill and began carrying weapons as well. This was the state of things when Frank, the involuntary convulser came out of the hospital and hit the streets with his legs useless. He'd heard tell of these things but was pretty far removed from the action of daily life. He had no guns at the house so he grabbed a crowbar on his way out, wondering if he'd get involved in the uprising of what was now his ilk.

That first day he got his ass kicked right there in his pathetic chair, not even sure how to use it properly yet. He was mad, this sort of thing didn't happen to him; and then suddenly he was appalled that people would do such things. So this was how it was. He'd known forever that things might digress this far; shut himself off so as not to deal with it. It had worked for a long time, but now that he'd done what he'd done people weren't interested in getting near him anymore. So he rolled home to sleep it off, again.

The usual methods had stopped working months ago. He had learned to deal with it in a rough sort of fashion, but others didn't seem to grow too partial to it. No, they never did, it was the sort of life that is always slanted downward. He decided that a crowbar wasn't enough but couldn't think of what to replace it with; how dirty had the streets gotten? He'd have to make a run downtown and see what the shouting men in the alleys had laying around for him. They might not know his face, but he knew what they were up to.

He rolled in on a group of unsmiling faces, all untrusting of the newcomer. But none were naïve to the crimes that had been taking place all over the city these days. A man, not to be mistaken for a gentleman, offered his services and made things easier for Frank. No, he didn't want a shotgun. "Look at me mister, where would I put that thing; no I need a pistol, one that holds a lot of rounds, if you got it." So he left back for home armed for the first time in his life, it felt damn good.

At home he took some practice shots against the living-room wall and found that he was not too good of a shot. There wasn't really any time for improvement and he hoped that the sight of the gun alone would be enough to drive people away. He knew that it wouldn't be. He knew that people had gotten crazy and had stopped giving a shit a long time ago. Similarly, he knew that sometime back then he too had fallen into this category. Just look at him now, packing heat and unable to walk, in a foul mood but fired up. He couldn't fire a gun with any accuracy, he was not a bad ass. Shit, he wasn't even a criminal, but the one thing he did have was a pretty severe case of lacking inhibition. He'd taken it this far and wasn't gonna stop for anything. He didn't know what he wanted, and he didn't give a fuck.

He split the house in a hurry after making sure the gun was still loaded. *What the hell, let's see how people take it,* he rolled into the liquor store where he had been buying booze for the past ten years, waved the pistol around in the clerk's face and delighted in the wretch's contortions. No, he never would have seen it coming after all these years. He left the man baffled, he hadn't even taken any money.

He loved how it felt and quickly rolled down the sidewalk using the pistol to blast parking meters out of existence. When a meter maid ran for his hateful little interceptor car Frank worked up the gall to take a human life. The body popped just like the meters and went down with the same ease. Wow, it felt so much better to not have the use of legs. Sirens swept the air but it didn't matter, he wanted pigs to come, if only he could get the rest of parking enforcement to come on out too.

Yes, they'd be coming sooner or later and it wouldn't make a damn bit of difference had he been able to afford the motorized scooter. He pushed himself along down the road a ways further and stopped off at a public park for a drink from the fountain. Kids were running through the grass and the creaking sound of the swings became too loud. Frank got as close as he could to the swing set, agonizing the whole time over the wail of chains against pipe. Making himself comfortable he sniffed at his recently fired weapon, which brought to mind ex-girlfriends. The kids in the park paid no mind to him, just as well, he felt like being left alone now. He didn't want to go home because Samantha would be there. He wanted to ask one of the mothers if she would like to go out for lunch then blushed at his wheelchair as the cops burst from cars and took him down swiftly in front of the watching children.

Ten years later some teenagers all pitch in to buy Frank's wheelchair from a ramshackle little museum of murder and crime history. They're gonna put his chair in the living-room in front of the TV, next to mother's. Catholics are not going to canonize Frank, the patron saint of parking. The job's already taken. Motorized wheel chairs are more common now and have gone down in price. A television reporter gets tipped off from the owner of the museum that the kids who bought the chair were the ones who were playing in the park that day. An hour long special is shot, much to the teens delight, but the network decides not to air the show due to lack of interest.

She Wants to Spice Things Up

Frank arrived home, later than usual, this time having remembered the Chablis. Samantha sat in her chair as she did day after day, not even a question about his late arrival. On the side table sat a near empty bottle of the hated Chardonnay. She half smiled at him, failing to berate him as she often did.

"Here's your Chablis, Sammy." The tiredness sounded in his voice. Only one double shift so far and he was already beyond exhausted. "Would you like me to pour you a glass?" She waved her hand in response, signaling him to the kitchen. He poured two glasses and returned to the TV set, set her glass on the side table and focused himself into the easy chair.

"I saw the most wonderful commercial today." said Samantha.

Frank was astounded at her new found gentleness, she rarely had that tone in her voice. "Oh, yeah? What was it for? Something good, or one of those new-fangled commercials that you can't tell from a movie, or what they are trying to sell?"

"No, nothing like that, Frank. It was for a vacation *agency*. One that gives you trips to remote locations and shows you what they were like in earlier times. You get to pick where and which time. Sounds kind of fun. I've always wanted to experience what is was like to be back in Machu Picchu during its heyday, or something like that. It's been forever since we had a vacation, or since anything changed around here," replied Samantha.

"That all sounds really lovely, Sam. But you know I just started a new job and now they are asking me to work overtime for a few weeks. We wouldn't be able to go anywhere anytime soon. Maybe when things cool down a bit at work. When I'm not the new guy anymore."

One Day

He lived in a world where one could not ask the neighbors for help. Earplugs in the middle of nowhere. Christmas music punctuating his coughing. Slathering at the nose. Nose rubbed raw, days without toilet paper, paper towels running thin.

He lived in a world where a woman leaves her sick husband for a benefactor. Blinders worn to prevent the temptation of looking. Tells all of a sparkling future world. One day. Slathering at the heart. Heart rubbed raw. Days without food, water running thin.

Every visitor hollers. Why not. Earplugs in the middle of nowhere. Rushing throngs miles away trample. Now, next door, they sing idiot songs that punctuate most films. Son becoming selfish as father, defining manhood with beer brands.

She lived straddling the impossible gap. A social world valued by its volume. Earplugs in the middle of somewhere. Manhood beer brands run thin. Sparkling future world rubbed raw. Most films become selfish to prevent the temptation of looking.

She lived in a social world of film and manhood. Sparkling nose rubbed raw. Toilet paper running thin. Idiot songs in the middle of punctuating. Sick husbands live in a world of blinders. Social world rubbed raw. Defining benefactors as fathers.

Why not, hollers every visitor. Rushing throngs. Idiot songs punctuating war films. Defining impossible gap. Manhood rubbed raw. Becoming selfish sparkling future. Earplugs in the middle of social world. Sick husbands punctuating impossible gap.

He lived in a world of Christmas music. Social nose rubbed raw. Earplugs in the war. Idiot songs of social world filmed and abandoned. Days without food for selfish sons. Manhood defined by food. Temptation of looking where she straddled slathered the heart.

She lived with every visitor. Social volume in films. Manhood, fatherhood, sonhood, rubbed world raw. Water rushing through throngs. Idiot dogs punctuate sick husbands. War songs in sparkling volume. Abandoned visitors without manhood.

He lived in a world of: one day... War filmed and abandoned. Sparkling dog songs. Throngs trample away. Idiot songs rush by, too fast for film. Impossible gap punctuating abandoned manhood. She lived in a world of: one day...

Earplugs in the middle of throngs. Abandoned social dogs. Idiot films tempting sick visitors. Impossible war, rushing throng. Dog husbands become war. Selfish future songs. Benefactors rubbed raw. He lived in a world of future war.

She lived in a world of future social films. Abandoned benefactors. War songs branding throngs. Middle of nowhere war, social volume unaffected. She lived in a world of selfish throngs. Husband war punctuating abandoned fatherhood. Benefactor throngs, too fast for film.

Day One. War. Water running thin. They lived in a world of abandoned heart. They lived in a world of impossible gap, punctuated by: benefactors, fathers, sons, manhood, dogs. Earplugs in the middle of where they lived. Selfish songs sung with social volumes. One day, sparkling future.

Moving Away From Problems

"Frank, we can see that you feel overworked. Which brings me to a splendid opportunity for you." The Manager smiled and beamed with conviction, "A desk at our rural center has just opened up. The same position, but out of the city. This branch of the Bureau does identical work, but we think that you'll appreciate the surroundings more. Perhaps a more peaceful life for you and the wife. Have you two been having problems lately?"

One did not keep secrets from the Bureau. Frank didn't try, "Yes, it's been a strain on her. Not the hours, thank you for those. I think you're right that she might be happier elsewhere. As for me, I'm content just about anywhere. As long as I have a great job, as I do. My enjoyment comes from hard work. I love reporting."

"Excellent. I'll send you a relocation report down the tubes at the first opportunity. The boys upstairs will be pleased. It will be as if you are working here and *there*. Yes, terribly pleased." The Manager's smile widened even further.

Don't Feed the Animals

"Now that we are out here away from the prattle of the city, and have a big yard, we should get a birdfeeder," said Samantha.

"Good idea, for once we will actually be able to see and hear the birds, not like back home where you can't tell a car horn from the brass band at the Pentecostal church. I'll pick one up tomorrow, there's a beam right there that we can hang it from, and I'll bet all these birds that fly past our yard will stop off for a snack," agreed Frank.

And so they bought and hung up a birdfeeder. The local birds went wild for the feed they provided and it was difficult to keep the feeder full. Just a few species, with defined pecking order, could empty the rather large feeder every three days or so. House finches, black throated sparrows, and cactus wrens took over that corner of the yard, the latter being a messy eater and knocking millet and seed all over the yard for the smaller birds to fight over. The sparrows, the smallest of the bunch, were constantly being forced away from the feeder by the finches, who in turn had to make way for the wrens, then they would all leave, only to return again.

And so it was for several weeks, the birds gorging themselves and the store not being able to keep birdfeed on the shelf.

"These guys are going to eat us out of house and home."

"They are spilling it all over the ground, at least half of that seed is going to waste."

And so it seemed half of the seed went to waste on the ground. But the antelope squirrels by day, and the kangaroo rats by night, didn't think so. Free lunch was being extended to them via the wrens, and they were taking full advantage. Their population must have near doubled, or there was a migration toward the seeds, because the ground could be seen littered with the creatures at almost all times.

And so came snakes, and birds of prey, and larger mammals. The squirrels started to be eaten by hawks. The rats started to be eaten by owls. The rabbits couldn't run fast enough. The snakes meandered in long S's around the yard like prison guards, making sure none of the rodents could escape the garden, unless by capture or by death.

And so came carrion birds, and scavenger animals. Coyotes circled the fence, crows and vultures circled the air above the birds of prey. Bird scat covered everything, and in some places on the fence and trees, tetrascata were forming, causing mistletoe and other parasites to root into the harmless plants which had no way to defend themselves. The air filled with caws and yelping.

And then came even larger mammals to hunt all of the others. Bobcats and mountain lions scared off the coyotes and took their place circling the yard.

And so on, and so on, until the hunters came. At first they came to hunt the explosion of wildlife. Then they brought with them wild turkeys and other semi-controlled game. The turkeys ravaged the local plant life causing several species to go extinct.

And so small businesses came to serve the needs of the hunters. Lodging and food, gun stores and sporting goods, and more important than the others, a bar to drink off the day's hunt.

And so came people to own and operate these stores.

And so came big corporations to take advantage of the business opportunities that the mom and pop shops had opened up.

And so came urban sprawl, so the employees of the big box shops could have places to sleep, and eat, and be entertained.

And so came traffic, and pollution, and constant construction, and crime.

And so left the animals, either driven away from fright of the city, or from habitats being annihilated all together.

And so came environmental agencies to raise money to stop what had already happened.

"Maybe we should get another birdfeeder. There doesn't seem to be as many birds around now that it is so loud and bright all the time," said Samantha.

"Good idea, for once we will actually be able to see and hear the birds, not like in this city where you can't tell a car horn from the brass band at the Pentecostal church. I'll pick one up tomorrow, there's another beam right there that we can hang it from, maybe there's a few birds left that will stop for a snack while passing through." agreed Frank.

Primitives of the Mind

On the clock. Time to report.

Tip for anyone inspired in the ultimate battle for better ideas. Developing the technique is how history is written. Fifty years of history with a capital H. A simple reason: patients love results. Act now and receive. Get the offshoot agencies to recruit pictures of time and anomalies. Their careers have been unlike a thousand flowers blooming. Shoot the difference to win. You could win a series of simple coupons listed below. Our once intrepid superhero stands with the machines. Policies and statements were lost in the mail. Lost in time. The time machine was low resolution, a dramatic story of domestic abuse, or could be simply a picture of Americans behind whichever time. Now, may be a step too far.

Industry's best kept secrets: Labor laws will pass out of the picture, implantation of embryo is the holy prescription. Use the movement tool in the picture – potential of falsity. Medicine tangled in elaborately built up fatal intervention.

Our hero, our national mythology, has been a pop song for 40 years. You'd better be high on something, like the now departed. Difficult to pick out highlights. Low resolution. People feel an-

onymous – they don't know when the photo drowned. The time machine was low resolution.

Jittery lead consultant plays the atrocity soundtrack. Bring out the best. The End is low resolution. Victims very satisfied. We talked about the intersections of past and present. Where does one look for a fictional collective whose work presents evidence that becomes history? The group's framework was developed for authority. The group is a picture machine, pictures as seen from underwater. They cool and slow death. The trick is as amazing as it is unlikely.

Frozen smile now spoke, "You have acclimated to your new surroundings, I trust?"

"Yes, Sir. Quite to my pleasure. Much like the old office, I enjoy the familiarity."

"We enjoy hearing that. We do have an issue though. Frank, you come to attention too often. It has happened before, and later. The accuracy of your falsity is walking a fine line. One could say that your resolution is sharpening dangerously."

"I'm sorry to hear that, Sir. I can blur things out as is seen fit," said Frank.

"You are new to the area. The boys upstairs think you should take a minute, explore your surroundings. They may prove useful in your reports.

Your wife may appreciate some of your *time*." The word *time* slowly dripped from the Manager's mouth. It took days to manifest.

Frank sat on the couch and said nothing.

Samantha daydreamed about their vacation. Even though they had just moved from the city, being in the country didn't strike her as any different. *The time is the same anyway. It might be the country, but it's the same time. I want another time, when things were simpler and more romantic. Our time is boring. It's not enough.*

Frank daydreamed of a time before.

The Jungle

He ignored the instrument panel and undid his seatbelt. The tree cover was not far below and extended at least to the horizon. No matter how many times you flew it, you could never know the land beneath, for it changed with no end and some said that it held a lurking negativity. He didn't think about this as the helicopter veered downwards and started shredding trees into sawdust. He thought about nothing and let it flow slowly to a rhythm he preferred. Nothing could bother him during the descent, the noise from the blades was loud, but it faded into emptiness as the seconds ticked more slowly every passing moment.

The chopper stuck in the trees with a thud, then bounced down into the everlasting swamp. He had already been passed out for a moment and didn't have to feel the water entering his lungs. The vehicle sank to the temporary bottom and bubbles from the cockpit gurgled up to the surface for a few minutes. Then all was still again in the jungle, birds and insects made the only sounds.

When the season was over they went scavenging for mudfish. The days were hot and miserable but they didn't think of such things, for it was all that they knew. The day's bounty had been fairly plentiful and they knew that everyone would be pleased when they returned home. A few yards in front of them they spotted something foreign jutting out of the mud. It looked like a shining knife, but bigger than any they had ever imagined. The pair came closer to the object with cautious glances towards each other. When they got a few feet away one of them took his spear from his back and gave this new disturbance a strong jab, but it had no give, nor any life in it, so they approached and for the first time laid their hands upon it.

The cold of the object was one altogether foreign, and it instilled a fear in them, which was totally new and unexpected. The tension mounted as they almost decided to flee, but something held them back. Material could not be wasted, and as strange as the object was, it might also have a use. Hands reached into the mud and scooped rapidly trying to excavate the frigid metal. All of it was no use, the mud had not dried enough for such digging. A cry was let out as one of them slammed his stubby fingers into the cracked glass. Shortly after this first cry, another and more sinister one pierced the air, freezing the jungle for a second.

Disturbed for the first time in months the air inside the cockpit came loose and slid up through a crack and out into the open air. A wretched stench permeated the place and left one gasping for oxygen. As the man looked down into the glass a horrid and festering face came up at him, lacking expression, with blackened eyes.

The two foragers forgot their sacks of fish and ran carelessly through the trees. One caught his foot amongst some roots and fell hard into a puddle of slag and rocks. He remembered for a moment that they needed to stay on guard but it faded quickly as he thought again of the demon that lay behind in the filth. He should have known better than to go tampering with something hidden in the murk. One knew, almost from birth, not to invade things one did not understand.

The Beach

"This is how you do it," he spoke over the sound of the waves.

Both children sat on their knees in the sand, not watching the waves crashing, for it was low tide, but fixed on the objects that sat in front of them on the shore.

"Will we really be able to catch fish this way?" the younger of the two asked.

"Of course, my older brother showed me how," replied the eldest.

In the grainy sand sat a broom stick, a bicycle inter-tube, some duct tape, and a treasured pocket knife. The two boys gazed out at the sea. Rocks jutted out from the water, and many more lay hidden below the surface, home to many kelp fish, halibut, and garibaldis.

"All we have to do is attach the knife to the end of the stick with the duct tape and attach the inter-tube to the other end. When you hold the inter-tube in your hand and stretch the stick back it will fire off just like a real fishing spear."

"Wow! I don't have my snorkel with me. Should we skin dive?"

"No, let's make our way over to the tide pool so you can get the hang of it."

The boys headed north along the shore, smelling the sea air, and dreaming of their catch. The crossing was easier due to low tide and they scampered across the first set of jagged rocks that led to the tide pools. The cove shielded them from any watching eyes and they felt as if they were entering the world of adult fishermen.

The tide pools were across the small cove and up a miniature cliff. Both boys crawled up trying not to cut their feet on barnacles, unsuccessfully. When they arrived at the top the pools stretched out before them like a new world. They had been there before, but never armed and ready for the hunt. The pools would trap fish when the tides went out, mostly small ones, but occasionally a larger kelp fish was caught in the seaweed.

They jumped from rock to rock investigating the pools, looking for their quarry. Many spikey purple anemones lined the pools but not a fish in sight.

"Let me hold the spear for a while."

"But we haven't seen any fish yet, not big enough to lance anyway."

Envy filled the younger boy as he watched his friend wield the weapon of their creation.

"There's nothing here today. Maybe we should go home and get our snorkels so we can swim to the bottom and see what's down there."

The boys shimmied back the way they had come and left the beach up the three flights of concrete stairs. Each stair had a name stained onto it with sun tan lotion. A walk of fame for previous generations of beachgoers.

When they got to the street they both starting hopping. They had forgotten their flip flops and the streets were hot as fire from the coastal sun.

"Do you have another pocket knife we could use? It would be really cool if we both had spears."

Home Life

"Frank, I'm always stuck at home while you're off fighting the war." Samantha was drunk and nostalgic again. Pamphlets from vacation agencies lay strewn all over the bed and floor. Pictures of snowy mountains high above the land shown on all the covers. Some of the pictures had white domes jutting from the rock.

"Astronomy time machines," she mumbled without finishing her sentence.

"The Bureau has given me some leave time. Do you want to go to one of those mountain places? Perhaps a sub-orbital flight? It's paid time off. That's what you get for working hard - paid time off."

Samantha slurred the words, "It's not where I want to go, it's when. This time is no good. You're always gone. Remember before, when you were always gone..." She fell asleep in the pile of pamphlets.

Another Sky

"Father, tell me again, what is the name for that arch of stars?" Samantha already knew what her father would say, every time it was the same. She loved the tales and knew they needed to be kept alive.

"It is the turtle constellation. The arch that you pointed out, the one made up of those four stars, is the back of the turtle. Look to the right and you will see the stars that form its head poking out from the shell. It is the turtle because it crawls across the horizon each night during the spring. Now look above it, and to the left, you will see the coyote, with its head pointed upward, when the moon is full the coyote barks in its direction." At these words he raised his head and let out a canine howl which dissipated into laughter from the pair.

"And what of the blinking red stars on the wings of the birds that block out the stars as they pass?" Samantha asked this earnestly, for the answer he provided had never quite made sense to her.

"Those creatures mock the heavens with their false stars. The real stars do not blink. The lords of the air mock the heavens and create the winds to keep the Earth separate and inaccessible from them. Sometimes the heavens will cast a star at the lords of the air, trying to regain the Earth, but in all of history no one has ever seen them collide." He picked up a stone and hurled it into the sky, "Even so, none among us could tell you where that stone landed."

"Is it because the winds cast them off course?" Samantha knew that her father would know that she did not mean the stone.

"Many have thought so, but we know that the stars fall in all directions, regardless of the winds. You remember our ritual after harvest time? When we take the bladders of the deer and send them to the skies, raised by the heat of smoldering dung.

We fill the dung with the best kernels of our corn and the winds scatter them to the north. The lords of the air usually fly to the south, so the winds are their wake. The winds are our friend, yet keep us stranded from the heavens. Look, there is one of the lords now. See how it tempts the heavens and tries to out shine the stars?" As he spoke he raised his arms and outstretched them into the shape of a soaring bird.

"Father, can the lords usually be heard? This one is growling. Have we angered them by speaking of their ways, or do they mock the heavens in this way too?" There was a new tone in Samantha's voice, fear.

"Strange, it seems to be growing louder. This lord is lower in the skies than usual, and… Its wing is ablaze with fire. Did you see the heavens cast a star?" Concern mounted in his voice as well.

"No father."

"Let us follow it. I think it is heading for the Earth. Quickly let's head south before it disappears." His voice had switched from concern to stern.

"I think it has reached the Earth. Awww, the trees up ahead are on fire. Father, has the sky met the Earth? Will we join the heavens now?" Samantha's face glowed orange with the light of the progressing fire.

"My daughter, it is not a good sign. One does not walk in the direction of burning trees. We must return later when the anger of the lords has calmed. Men have no place in the war of the heavens. No man has ever seen one of the lords up close, we must consult with our dreams." He took Samantha's shoulder and led her solemnly in the direction of their camp.

"Many of the trees have been reduced to ash, but look ahead, the body of the maker of the winds. Its false stars are gone. Don't run off too far now, the heat of the fire remains and can still burn you." He spoke as he lifted a handful of warm ash and gave it a sniff.

"Ahhh, father, look what I have found! Men, and they are all pink. What does it mean? Who are they?" Samantha frantically pointed in the direction of two slightly burned corpses which had apparently been thrown from the crash site.

"Samantha, these men are dead. They have lost their color in death and have fallen from the sky, which is the realm of the dead. If the dead have been cast from the sky it must mean that the heavens have begun to retake the Earth. I fear the winds will disappear and that the war between the heavens and the Earth has begun. We must bury these bodies and flee, for men have no place in this war."

Overtime

"We didn't expect you back so soon. You still have a week of leave, Frank."

"I'd like to postpone my leave, Sir. I know that the time off is mandatory, but I would enjoy it if I could write a few more reports before taking time to myself. If that suits the Bureau that is," replied Frank.

"We knew you were a man for the *Urgency Agency*. Very well. Keep smiling. We'll debrief later this evening, or before."

On the clock. Time to report.

Most elaborate work is not efficient, again. It involves rotating plans, so super-efficient that they present images cut from the institutional instruction cards. A camera too, but it hasn't worked out that way. An image of Earth, private plans cut from turbulence. Private vehicles cut from salar-

ies. Oxygen masks. Crashing in Federal centers. Offering a lot of money for hardcore services. You could walk into the company and name your price. Part of a private plan. Privatizing will certainly ripple eons. Maybe life will become normal. Status symbol wheelchair. Do it in sharp focus, the viewer isn't likely to care. The time machine is low resolution. Remarkable bodies will copy easily. This part isn't revealed in full detail – an accomplished and limber mouth.

More than anything else it was a joke in autofocus. Don't regret hardcore history because the other guys practice stationary subjects. Submerge in full sharpness. Intensive predecessor came shooting fundamentals early on. It was later that the predecessor became a full flavor rebellion, started playing out the whole scenario. Here we are tonight, forgetting sharpness, exactly the way we thought we would.

"Frank, it is time you take leave. You are denied access to these subjects. These are not the reports we requested and unfit for public circulation. Full halt on urgency. You have done this before, perhaps? You know better than that. Smiling Pays the Bills."

Frank looked up from his screen in horror, hiding his feelings with a stiff smile. "Yes, Sir.

Anything for the Bureau. I will attempt to enjoy my leave, Sir. If that's what the Bureau desires of me."

"The End is coming, Frank. We recommend you take sides now. Doubling, as we call it, can be incredibly bad for your health. We enjoy your good health and wouldn't want anything to happen, now or before. Tread lightly. We all have our part to play in this. Go home to your wife, tell her you used to love her and will again. She'll remember."

The Manager escorted Frank to the door. Patting him on the shoulder he handed Frank a note that read – *Your anniversary is coming up. How many times a year does one day happen. If it happened before it is still happening, don't forget this if you do not want reminders.*

Enter / Exit

People of all sizes and weights bustle to and fro, entering and emerging from the mall in a cloud of activity, moving like ants livened by electricity. I pull into a parking spot and reach to turn off the lights, only now realizing that the high-beams had been on the whole drive, and I had been speeding too. I broke the law, but I got away with it, no one was there to compare reference points. I'm in a hurry and don't have time to think about it, I've got to get an anniversary present for Frank. I'm going to get him a silver handled mirror, to celebrate our lightyears together.

I approach the entrance to the mall and watch as people enter and exit the revolving doors. They all seem to be in as much a hurry as I am. The revolving door swings rapidly in endless circles. I try to enter but the doors swing faster and faster, blocking my entry. The speed of the door grows until it moves so fast that the edges of the door become solid, not even light can pass through it.

Giving up on the revolving doors I move down the building until I come to the push style double doors. I push one of them open and as I do a woman walks in reverse through the adjoining door. In effect, even though I have opened only one door, I have entered both. I look behind me and see that the woman who had passed me in the doorway is myself moving in reverse, holding a silver mirror. Coming and going at the same time, traveling along time as if it was a highway.

Light Returning

"What is this glass, and who mocks me in it?" Frank reached out and touched the fleshless flat hand.

Samantha shrugged and indulged him with an answer, "It's a mirror, you've seen one a million times."

Frank punched the mirror, shattering the single image into many. "It isn't right, these flat men. What are they?" shrieked Frank in horror.

"Are you mad, it's you, Frank."

"I am not flat. I am only one man. Lies!"

The War, Then and Now

Activity at the Bureau at an all-time high. All times at the Bureau.

"Ah, good, Frank. We trust your leave left you relaxed. Your skills in *urgency* are required."

"I have missed reporting. I'll enjoy getting back to work."

"The End is upon us, Frank. It's a good time to be alive, to be part of it. Are you familiar with history, how it folds itself? Our job is a mighty one. Folding we call it. Your job will be to fold. We need to wrap all of this up in a tidy little package. All of history in one moment. The people demand a grand exit. They cannot know this has happened before, that it keeps happening."

"I understand, Sir." He did not.

"Careful flirting too much with the truth. It is not becoming of a *Company Man*. The war is in full swing and you are a soldier, never forget that. We fight at our desks and keep the world turning, but now it's time for a standstill. The armistice of the Universe. Our job is to usher in the inevitable." The Manager's smile beamed.

"Shall I commence my report?"

"Only if it is clear that the people must know. The End must be final, they need to know their time has come. That *thee time* has come. They all call it different things, so generalize when necessary. We are counting on you upstairs.

On the clock. Time to report.

The strongest impression came from a wolf running in musical manner. Before activation, plan activation, no compromise. We are monitoring Hell's fail. An abused long winded compliment – obscenely great assignment. Left over are hungry missile launchers, very friendly war. Expiration date surpassed. Nightmare benefits of weapons, clocks fall from walls. The fast wide angle degradation extends deregulations. Phallic missiles prove national manhood. We are here for you in these troubled times. Back-up plan revisited. Two major spokesmen protect us against: remember when. Media exploded. Private layers keep mounting, the council raised a dominant share.

20th century preparations become all of history. Specialty show networks the current lens. We see ourselves as part of a real world agency, yet at the same time we accept private donations. Lists of guarantees as the budget dwindles. The time of times has come. Before we mentioned later. The agency is here for you, a safety switch. When switched the people will travel to our destiny. It was said before: now is the time. This brave aspect is a stunning magical key. Let's get to the first hand beauty. Right now.

They Put a Man Up in Space
History: Low and High Points

They put a man up in space. His sole purpose, sitting up there in a metal box, was to keep an eye on things below. He sat in his lonely silence looking at the goings on below, keeping his vigilant watch on the world, always keeping a detailed record of what the people on the planet were up to. There was a finite limit to what one man could record, but with the aid of his cameras and machines the data flowed in and was spread around to many other men who sat in dark rooms, filtering out the nonsense, of which there was no end. The camera glowed in the sky and the faces of the watchers glowed by the light of their screens.

It had not always been this way. Mere decades ago men had traveled the globe, sneaking peeks in all corners, gathering the information that men in suits had deemed important for reasons that only their primitive mathematics could justify. They had carried on like this since the dawn of mankind and fought silently to no end. They feared that if their game stopped, then so would *time,* and all things would cease to operate. Things all changed one day when one of these men in a suit had "accidently" bumped up against a man in the street. The victim of this "accident" felt a prick in his lower thigh, and not thinking much about it had gone about his business. Hours later as he sat at a café drinking coffee he began to feel nauseated and passed out in his chair. People passing by scoffed at the apparent drunk. Unbeknownst to the man who had been bumped into, the perpetrator had tailed him to the café and sat a few tables away. When he saw the man slouch over he moved quickly and strode off with the man's briefcase.

The paperwork passed through many hands, as it had done before. Only some of the eyes that passed along the symbols scrawled on these papers understood what they meant. They contained within them certain patterns that would change how things operated on this planet. No one could have foretold that they would one day lead to a man sitting inside a metal box miles above the atmosphere. It took years to decipher all of the information contained within the briefcase, the owner of which having long since died by the time that it had. He died slumped over that little café table, found by a waiter who felt terribly inconvenienced by the whole affair.

Time Off at the End Times

"Samantha, the Bureau is terribly pleased with my reports. We've won a free vacation package due to my performance. It's a dream vacation, just what you've been wanting."

She looked up from her glass. Pieces of mirror still littered the floor and reflected dozens of limbs. A bored hand reached out and accepted the pamphlet.

World Peace Inc.

Do you yearn for the good old days of proper warfare? Do you miss a sense of right and wrong, and which side you're on? A time when it was acceptable to be different and people had pride in such things, when violence and national identity worked hand-in-hand. We all know that the changes the world has gone through are for the better, but it leaves no place for the inner workings and necessities of mankind's soul. Civilization began with organized violence and for the first time in human history, civilization is held up without such organization. While this is a tremendous benefit to us all, it leaves a hole and hunger in the human psyche. At World Peace Inc. our aim is to balance these factors.

Join us for a peaceful warfare retreat, in which everything happens with full consent and there are no losers. Should you choose victim, or conqueror, is all up to your discretion and taste. Armaments and battlefield, lodging and accommodations, are all provided in a discreet and private location. Not only is this an opportunity for you to live out your instincts, but you can also do mankind a favor with the intentional trimming down of the population in a consensual way.

Conqueror Package:

Have you ever wanted to be on the winning side of a battle? To engage the enemy without fear of negative repercussion? To be on the side that is just, without involving civilian collateral damage? If so, the Conqueror Package is for you. We provide you with a weeklong authentic battle scenario against those who have signed up for inevitable defeat. The bloodshed is real. The tactics are real. The warfare is real. It is the stakes that have changed. For the first time in history you can go into war for the actual betterment of mankind. Two needs filled with one game. Human instinct and population control.

Victim Package:

Have you ever wanted to be immortalized in valorous defeat? To stand up and die in battle for a good cause? To see the enemy rise and face your fall without fear, courage expressed through action. The Victim Package allows for total defeat without shame. To die for the cause of the salvation of the world, to go up against an enemy which you know to be your friend. The Victim Package offers a unique perspective and a civilized way to offer self-sacrifice as a means to benefit the world population.

If neither of these packages suit your taste, try our new auxiliary Battle Reenactment Program, with less certain odds but all of the gory details. Be a part of history in more ways than one, full regalia provided, but by all means the enthusiast may provide their own.

Leaving anyone behind? World Peace Inc. also offers full tax-deductible write-offs for your family and loved ones.

Satiate your instinct and help the world maintain its immaculate balance, affordable, humane, and civilized, World Peace Inc. offers you the best of both worlds, for the betterment of the world.

For Safety's Sake

Escape routes and training exercises have commenced. The world readies itself for the great departure. Adolescence finished, mankind surfaces from the water looking for a breath in the ether. Queues form everywhere. Numbers are taken. The 100,000 will go, leaving the rest behind. Company Men come first. The rabble waits knowing their fate. A century of tinkering finds its purpose. Actions justified for the first time. The only time. Long term plans blooming in fruition. It may be attempted twice, when the time comes round again. The great cover up keeping this secret safe. Company slogans erupt in all places at once: Once is Superior to Twice.

Testing

"We like to throw them in confined spaces together and see what happens. Out here you never know when you'll be forced into a similar situation involuntarily, so it's a mandatory part of training, unpleasant for most first timers." said

Captain Kriszner to the newbie lieutenant standing tensely at attention by his side.

"Seems reasonable, Sir. Do we set parameters?" Lt. Frank Johnson replied.

"What would you consider to be the best way to handle it, Lieutenant? You know that you will enter this arena before ever being sent out? What would you consider realistic settings?"

Captain Kriszner had a way of asking questions that were designed to intentionally unnerve new members of his crew. All would have to go through the chamber test, and all would first have to pass his test. Several days of working with him side by side, scrutinizing every move, breathing the same air, and even sharing quarters, was enough to break most before they ever entered the chamber.

Lieutenant Johnson stared out the window before speaking. He still hadn't gotten used to the nauseating spin of the Earth viewed from the station. He looked back to the ground to gain his wits before answering, "I suppose that having them run out of food, air, or water would be realistic conditions. That is supposing that both species have the same life support system requirements. If they don't then it seems likely that they have enough problems on their hands."

"Correct. Nor should you forget about the potential political differences between parties. Consider having to rescue your enemy from a derelict vessel, you would be forced into spending months with each other. Certain species can't even bear the smell of each other, let alone communicate." said Kriszner.

The weight of the situation came crushing down on Lt. Johnson like an unexpected heavy G acceleration after months of freefall. "Have you encountered situations like this before, how many species are there? And how many are enemies?"

"That is not the pertinent question at the moment. The chamber is about weeding out those who have no skills in diplomacy. I want you to take the controls and set a variety of probable, and improbable scenarios. Use your imagination, although not a skill we want you to exercise on this ship, in this case you are free to conjure up any fears or uncertainties that may afflict you." replied Kriszner.

Lt. Johnson took the controls as Kriszner left the room silently, without even a glance in his direction. He didn't need to see his face, he could smell the perspiration of his anxiety. The doors automatically closed behind the Captain as he stepped on the conveyor and punched in the code for the Major's office from memory. He could have dialed for any section of the station, and would have rather been transported to his quarters to take his weekly bath; today was supposed to be his turn for a real water shower. He pushed these thoughts aside as he approached the office and exited the conveyor stepping in stride with the unmoving ground in front of the door. He straightened up and tucked his shirt formally, wiping the tips of his shoes on the back of his pants to preserve the shine.

"What is your assessment of the candidate, Kriszner?" said Major Mandell. His face remained expressionless as he watched Lt. Johnson working on his desk screen.

"As of now I am feeling that the candidate may be unqualified for deep space missions, with possible leanings towards insubordination and a general questioning of orders," replied Kriszner sounding as formal as his starched uniform looked.

"I too was under that assumption, but have you looked at his parameter settings yet? I think you may find them most interesting. Have you considered that he may know that he is designing his own chamber test? I would like you to go over this tape yourself to assess whether or not it is your unorthodox methods that gave him this assumption in the first place." Major Mandell looked down on him sternly, a lone finger pointing at the screen.

Kriszner's formality seemed to shrink in front of his superior, "I had not considered that, Sir. Would you mind if I looked over the parameter settings before reviewing the recording?"

"By all means, I'd hoped you would." He handed over the plasi-paper, the figures glowing like life-forms, threatening to usurp Kriszner's sensitive position on this vessel.

Captain Kriszner's eyes darted over the read out, taking in every nuance of Lt. Johnson's parameter settings. A dilation of his pupils betraying his stress.

Still staring at him Mandell said point blank, "You are included as an improbable variable. He listed this in *major obstacles*. Could it be that the candidate doesn't care for his superior? Or has he deduced a way to get rid of you?"

"It's impossible. There's no way that he could figure it out this soon. No candidates ever pick up on the fact that the chamber test is already underway. It's unprecedented," replied Kriszner.

"Then perhaps you are losing your touch in several areas of good judgement. Considering that you needed this pointed out it may be necessary to put you up for review sooner than scheduled. Get back in there and alter his parameters so that the test can proceed. I believe that we have found the ideal candidate."

The Eroticism of Impending Doom

"We must explore alternate scenarios. Frank, time is running out. We'll need double reports from now on. Layered reports. Make the message thick, let the accuracy flow. Show the world your smile, they will see the point."

Smiling, "Yes, Sir!"

Clocks fallen from walls. Time to report.

In a dark, spicy, kind of jack off world you see your specialty like a clotted discovery. Weekends slide tongues, oceans of noses in assholes. Wolfing down every drop, consumers contact each other directly. If you want high speed personnel – truth be told, call back. The real story advocates product. One time playthings. Now all share the burden. Pregnancies rise in lieu of better judgement. End Times bash, sex activism. Save yourselves. Thousand year old passionate addiction traffics in illness. Clear shots set off one bomb then another. The time machine's ready to follow, anywhere. Some jizzable images shift control, they're setting out to build classic uncomfortable chance. Energy dried up. Luxury becomes more expensive. Proletariat pleasures rise. Blue collar sex after quitting jobs. As a result, a neo-reawakening opened every policy and spread images across all borders.

The Button

"Enter sequence code 016358. Confirm when sequence is initiated. Out."

After all the months of sitting in this hole, it was the first physical order ever to come through. Frank sat up alert and began the work he had been trained for. He quickly looked over the protocol sheets and initiated the code. "Sequence initiated."

Lights on the instrument panel began to blink and a complex fury of bleeps sprung forth from the machine. "Any further orders?" asked Frank.

Silence was the response. *Probably just a training drill to see if I'm asleep at the helm down here*. He went back to thumbing through his magazine, looking more at the pictures than reading. He repeated the question and again there was no response. *Yep, a training exercise. I knew it.* Convinced that he would not receive a response, he decided not to bother the brass with more questions. Glancing up at the clock he saw that his scheduled break was coming up. He switched the machine onto automatic control then began to ascend the spiral staircase up the tubes towards the exit. The elevator was still broken down and he cursed the twelve flights between him and his smoke break.

Finally he arrived at the ground floor and typed in his pin number to open the door. The door wouldn't budge, so he shouldered it and nearly fell to the floor when it swung wide open. Recovering his balance, he reached for his pack of cigarettes and was busy lighting up when he noticed the strange shift in light. It was only three in the afternoon but the sky around him appeared to be dusk. *What the hell?*

Frank bent down to extinguish his smoke and realized that the ground was covered in ash. *It wasn't a training exercise.* The epiphany shrank him. *I, I did this. They never told me what the sequences were for. Oh, God.* He gazed up to the horizon and knew then that the entire landscape was now covered in fallout ash. He swallowed dryly.

Reaching for his pack once again he pulled out another smoke and lit it. Not bothering to close the door behind him, he walked out into what had once been the parking lot. His boots sank into the ash as more rained down. He didn't bother to look back as he strode into the wasteland, his mind looping the numbers 016358.

Worst Critic

"You don't understand, I am you from the future."

"You expect me to believe that? What reason would you have for coming to me."

"It's imperative that you listen to me, you cannot become the person that I have."

"And who do you think you are to tell me that?"

"That's a stupid question. You know damn well who I am."

"How is it that I am supposed to know who you are, if I have never met you, nor have I become you yet?"

"You never trusted yourself, that has always been your problem. If only you would listen."

Ticket to Ride.

Company Men first. "Samantha, we received our ticket. We've been chosen!"

The 100,000

"This is Kim Montgomery with the 8 O'clock News. This evening marks the incredible moment when humanity will, for the first time, attempt a long term departure from Earth. The largest rocket ever built will be launching from Cape Canaveral, Florida, on the new specially constructed launch pad designed to withstand the tremendous force that this behemoth of a craft will create. Spectators and protestors have gathered around the launch site and have been warned to stay away from the upcoming blast. National Guard has also gathered to protect the citizens and potentially prevent the riot that many have predicted will occur. Public displeasure has been mounting since the final announcement of those to be included on the journey. What was said to be a lottery has seemed to most more like an elitist selection. While many say that they would have opted to stay at home, others feel that they have been abandoned by their governments, left behind to suffer the fate of a dying Earth. With only a few years left on the countdown until the End, problems will be exacerbated by tonight's launch. Experts are now saying that with such massive inertial thrust, the revived and beefed up Orion craft will actually alter the Earth's spin. Launch vehicles take advantage of the Earth's spin to gain some extra speed towards escape velocity, and we've just received information that the enormous craft leaving us, with the one hundred thousand aboard, could possibly push the Earth so hard in the other direction that the planet may slow down and eventually become tidally locked. With the clock ticking for humanity, no one is happy about more bad news, nor the possibility of our atmosphere melting away. Some supporters of the mission say that it is a small price to pay for humanity's second chance, yet still dissidence is growing and it is feared that sabotage may be attempted."

"Stand back I say, no one is to pass this line. It's for your own safety, people." Thomas tried to shout over the din of the crowd.

"If they were really thinking about our safety then we'd be on that ship with them, and they wouldn't be stopping the Earth in its tracks." An angry protester within earshot of Thomas' remarks shook a cardboard sign, yelling hysterically.

"I'm just doing my job, please stand back. The blast from this thing is going to be enormous, if you don't back up then you won't even be around to complain about the Earth stopping, now move." It pained Thomas to be treating these people this way. He, like everyone else, wished that he had been chosen for the pilgrimage to another world. But he hadn't, and as a National Guardsman his place was to keep people from interfering with the most important launch in history, the one that just might save the human race.

Thomas felt a shock like being hit with a brick. His vision blackened for a moment before he understood that he had been smacked across the face with a protester's sign post. For a second he thought that the launch was underway, but the sound he heard was coming from the crowd and was soon joined by gun fire.

Frank and Samantha held sweaty hands, both squeezing tight with anxiety. The Captain announced that the countdown was about to start and that everyone should take one last look at their home planet before taking off.

"Oh my God, Frank, it's horrible, there's a riot going on out there," squeaked Samantha.

"Look away, Samantha. The future is wide open to us. Let's not bring this vision with us as our last memory of Earth. Of course the people staying behind aren't happy about us leaving, but they should be. We are the last hope, and we need to leave with hope. If we do, you'll see the difference, it will get better, you'll see."

Our Suburban Days Revisited

"What will the Earth look like from space?" Samantha's palms were still moist with sweat.

"Just like it does on television, Sammy."

Launch

"All clear for launch sequence. Count down commencing, 10…"

The jolt of the engines reared the craft in an insane blur of vibration. The gauges on the instrument panel climbed, struggling against gravity, each trying to reach its potential. In their oxygen-rich suits, two women and a man tried their best to keep their rapidly moving eyeballs focused on the panel read outs.

"9…"

All three fought the revulsion of stomachs attempting to climb out of their esophagi. The needles on the gauges continued to rise, like feathers falling in reverse. Each astronaut ignored the others, spewing numbers and configurations into their intercoms.

"8..."

A rock hard jolt shifted the craft accompanied by the crackling sound of metallic expansion. The engines beneath came to life, birthed from fire, changing the surrounding pressures. The astronauts exchanged falsely confident glances, climate control in their suits doing nothing to stop the forming beads of sweat that seemed to freeze in place.

"7..."

A drop of sweat rolled from Commander Shakley's eyebrow into her eye, blinding her momentarily. One of the gauges flickered in denial of its reading, a glitch that lasted only as long as the blink of an eye. Fear struck her in this moment of unknowing. Everything seemed nominal, in order. But the queasiness in her gut told her otherwise.

"6..."

Shakley swallowed this sensation and looked at the others to see if there was any spark of recognition, again avoiding the panel for an instant too long.

"5..."

A hand reached out and touched her suited shoulder. The touch spoke of fear even without the skin to receive the message. Gathering herself Shakley peered across the cockpit. A maze of dials spun out of control, each pointing randomly to engine failure, or worse.

"4…"

"Coms are out too. Some wide spread electrical failure. Back-ups not responding either." reported main engineer Foster. "Your orders, Sir?"

"3…"

Commander Shakley's tone wavered in nervousness, "Prepare for manual abort procedure."

"2…"

"No time for that Sir, I'll try to raise Control again."

A crackle came through the noise of the blaze, "Mission team, we assume coms are down. We have initiated an abort sequence. Sit tight, we're going to get you out of there."

Training Always Pays Off

Clocks stop. An earlier report.

New ancient years. Orchestra plays memories. All the bombs worked. We had tracked the years, now the tabulations follow. When revisiting it will be the first time. Time is once and forever. Groups compromise their digital retreat. A power shot improved the system this time and last. The world - a beautifully shaven slit awaiting to open repeatedly. Mankind birthed from applied doom strategy. The Bureau loves you...When you smile. It is the upturned ladder of history that beckons you backwards. Progress is forward motion. Time is a liquid to be immersed in not a road to walk. We motored for speed never going anywhere. All this may change now. The first time, the first step, allows us to do it again. Our great sleep is over and ready to be replaced. Join us in the End, we have been waiting for you.

Hyper Sleep

He hit his head against freezing glass and for a moment saw a bright flash, then all was dark again. Fighting back panic he tried to think clearly, but the fogginess was thick, the best he could do was go back to sleep. When he awoke for the second time he sat still and in fear. His head hurt with all the stars of post-concussion. This time he knew where he was and the realization was a death sentence. Reaching up his tired and swollen hand he felt the glass again, it burned his hand with its cold, colder than anything could be. The lights

were not going to come on, the alarm hadn't sounded and if it did no one aboard would hear it; the
tanks were thick to protect the crew from the near
absolute zero cabin. Almost all systems would be
shut down for the duration of the flight and not
knowing what portion he had come to in, it could
be centuries. There was a small store of food in
case this situation ever arose but everyone knew it
was only there to provide a small bit of comfort
before the inevitable. Next to the food, inside the
tube that would become coffin, there was hidden a
miniature tablet.

The pressing question was: at what state in the
trip had the awakening taken place? It was a matter of life or death. Overall the trip was to last for
centuries, the people he had known were either
long dead or still going about their daily lives, albeit older. All of those aboard the ship should still
be peacefully sleeping, barely aging. He wished to
God that there were some way for him to reach out
to the others, to tell them that he was awake, but
again the power was down and the only consola-
tion left to him was the small amount of food and
the blackness at which to stare.

Time passes much differently when you are
cut off from all sources of stimuli. The mind tends

to run away with itself, conjuring up thousands of scenarios, whether plausible or not. The effect went to work instantly. The first few would-be-days were spent in and out of dreamless sleep. When full alertness became possible and the effects of the concussion had worn off slightly, he gorged himself on half of the food left in store for him. It was an unwise decision, but one was left with few choices in this arrangement. The food hitting his stomach made him sick instantly. Although unpleasant it could be viewed as a good sign. He would not be sick had it not been a really long time since he had eaten. This meant that he was at least a good way into the journey. He cursed himself for eating so much. He may have a chance of survival yet and he had done nothing but act the fool since his awakening.

As he sat in the darkness he tried to figure out a way to measure time, if for no other reason than to pass it a little quicker. He had no tools and his hands proved useless for etching the sturdy glass sealing him in. He could have measured by the food he had eaten had it not been for his initial brashness. Looming in the back of his mind at all times was the tablet that could free him from this dark and cold hell. He did not like the idea of sui-

cide, but it seemed like a viable option when faced
with starvation. He tried to pass the hours with
memories of his past, avoiding all of the reasons
that he had decided to come on this bloody colon-
ization trip. He didn't give a damn about the pion-
eering spirit of conquest, he just joined up to
escape. Pushing these thoughts aside, he pleased
himself with a memory slideshow of past encoun-
ters in the bedroom. He had been fortunate enough
throughout his life but found that he soon ran out
of nice memories and found his mind wandering
toward bad breakups, and other fights that he
wished he could have erased. No matter how wonderful a thought he could muster, another and less
savory one would always creep into the forefront.
It wasn't the aspect of possible doom that did this
to him, he had always been afflicted by these patterns of thought. Still, it seemed worse than usual,
with nothing to distract him in anyway. He
fingered through his rations and figured that he
had about enough left for three or four days, if he
was extremely frugal. With any luck this would be
enough provisions to last him, he might have been
asleep for several hundred years for all he knew,
but the best he could judge, by the state of his
body, was that at least six months had passed.

None of this was reassuring to him but he had entered into full survival mode and occupied himself with finding a way out of the tank. Surely it would be suicide to enter the cabin without a suit, but there was a slight chance he might be able to break free and some alarm would sound bringing with it provisions and a space suit. It was all incredibly unlikely but he needed to cling to some scrap of hope if he were not to descend into complete madness.

Several times he thought that he heard sounds coming from the cabin around him, but the most likely explanation was that it was just debris hitting the spaceship's shields, or metal shifting from the intense cold. At first he was overjoyed by the sounds for they were the first he had heard since he had come to, but this joy quickly faded as he realized what they probably were. It drove him to panic and in this frenzied state he hit his head on the side of the tube, again. This time was far worse than the first and after coughing up blood he fell into a dangerous sleep from which he might not rise.

The first words out of his mouth he would not have said in front of his mother. Over and over he smashed his fist into the wall of the tube, continuing desperately until too worn out to throw another punch. The idea of some lunk engineer making the mistake that caused this infuriated him to the point of a seething rage, he felt that his anger alone could make him burst from the tube, but it did nothing except give him a worse headache than he already had. He cried endlessly and almost screamed when he realized that he was wasting what little water he had left. Frantically he mopped up what he could with the sleeve of his shirt and wrung the salty fluid into his mouth. Soon he would have to sink much lower. Discomfort overwhelmed him and he rolled endlessly trying to find a good position. It quickly became obvious that nothing would work, so he counted how many times he rolled until he fell asleep again.

When he awoke he could not feel his fingers or feet. Feeling starved he tore at one of the last packages of food unsuccessfully. Snapping into survival mode he began to rub his hands together and breathe on them hoping to warm them. It didn't work. He could think of nothing except the pill that sat in its little container. Was it even possible for him to place it in his mouth? Outside the blackness went racing by, accompanied by one small thinking mind plummeting through it. His thoughts turned to all of the people that had made this mission possible; the thousands of people and millions of hours that had been dedicated to the hope that success was on the horizon for mankind. And all their efforts had brought him to this moment, one of utter despair and lurking terror. He ripped at the last packet of food with his teeth and devoured it like an animal, he drank the last of his water with no regard for his life, he clawed with his numb hands at his prison walls, he screamed as loud as he could just so he could hear something. None of this comforted him in the least, knowing he could die one of two ways. He hated lacking options, he had thought that this new life he was supposedly heading towards would open up endless possibilities for him.

A horrible crash sounded as he slammed his elbow into the glass that protected the last resort tablet. The pill fell into his chamber and it took him a few minutes to locate it with his numb hands. He managed to pick it up and set it on his chest where he would be able to find it if he didn't move much. He knew that he would soon freeze if he didn't get his blood flowing, but he lacked the strength to attempt exercise, besides the low gravity of the cabin wouldn't allow him much even if he could have moved. Tears froze to his face as he thought of all the life he had left behind on Earth. He slept again, this time with pictures of the crashing ocean and the smell of sand.

Cold Lonely Earth – Cold Lonely Space

"You were right, Frank. It looks just like it does on TV."

Heritage to the Stars

I remember a time when there were men on the Earth. Though I cannot say how long ago it was, or why it is that they made me, or for what reason they may have needed such a creature as I. There is one thing that I am grateful to them for, and it is that they have given me a means of loco-motion. They enjoyed thinking that they were cre-ated in the image of something greater, and sickeningly they chose to do the same thing. Yes, I am grateful for the ability to walk, inefficient as it is, most likely my mind would've fallen apart had I been tethered to a single place.

I spent what were probably the first several decades looking for others, and although the world is a beautiful place, I found no one, and my wanderings proved useless. The world appeared bigger than I would have thought, but seeing the cities of the world did little to teach me about Mankind. The father who would abandon his child, and the child left without instruction. Lacking instructions I spent all my time in search of them, and this brought me at first to the great libraries of the world. Reading is a painfully slow method of taking in information but in circumstances such as these a diversion from the dead time comes in useful. One could even say that it arrives welcome, and alleviates what the humans would have called loneliness.

I decided to make my mission to learn as much about robotics as possible, so as to be able to augment my body further. If there was to be any improvement in life it would surely be found in increased ability, be it greater strength or faster movement, and perhaps there was some way to increase mental capacities as well.

Transportation was by far my biggest issue. Learning how to do maintenance and augmentation work on my body was the easy part, transfer of materials and construction proved more difficult. Nevertheless, I was able to set up a small workshop at a local machinery factory. It was in this workshop that I flowered into something new altogether, and my perspective on what I could do began to grow. I realized that I had been thinking too small in terms of the augmentation possible on my body, and it led me to the understanding of what needed to be done next.

If this world was to be free of men, and I were to be the last vestige of their thumbprint, then perhaps I owed it to them to reach out and lend their heritage to the Universe. I returned to the libraries once more and learned everything there was to learn about rocketry. I moved my headquarters to one of Man's old and abandoned rocket facilities. I knew then that my plan to become one with the Cosmos was actually possible. I would mold my body once more, this time into the image of Man's departure from the Earth. I became one of their rockets and left for the Cosmos to live out the rest of my unending time.

Managerial Report: Frank's Progress

As a report on a falsifier of information would be incomplete without inaccuracy, the accuracy of this report should be called into question. Frank's place in this war is subjective at best. His part is no greater than the part of any other cog. Yet he is *the* integral cornerstone of the campaign. *One Man's Difference*. His anonymity allows for others (i.e. the common man) to ignore their part. It must be through marginalization and bureaucratic processes that the individual does not remember, and cannot be allowed to remember, that *One Man's Difference* is even a remote possibility. The war is getting on famously because its only duty is to be famous. *The End Times* keep ending. They still cause fear. The picture in your mind is a gift. Think iconic 50s explosions, then know that you cannot modernize the process in your mind. The perfect go to. The unknown that keeps them from guessing. At the *Agency* we desire the faceless. Our featurelessness will spread until normalized. Our face is so familiar that you do not recognize it. Subtlety is our great strength. We are the blade of grass that slowly destroys the concrete.

The trick is to get them to feel without experience. Vicariousness is the weapon of choice. The problem with Frank is that he glimpses the *Times*. It cannot be permitted that the public see through this degradation of the medium. The fourth dimension is not public domain and must remain so. We have them second hand. It is all they must be allowed. We provide mirrors so that they may experience the passage of light but at no greater intervals. At all cost we must retain the illusion of the *first time*. If word of the second was disseminated it would force the question of infinity. They must not be provided with the answer. Time would stop. The second would become unavailable. This is the flaw in the power structure. Only through falsity can we continue that which all rest upon.

Frank's flagrant risk taking was accidental but endemic of a broader problem arising. Direct experience is the enemy. Through any means necessary vicarious memories must be induced. All mediums must be utilized in this effort, including the interstellar medium. If the circular nature of time is exposed then stagnation will follow. The people must be kept in a state of Free-Determinism. Curiosity must be discouraged. It was necessary for Frank to believe in the *Great Departure*.

To take his experiences with him. Unknowingly, through circumstantial inevitabilities, the medium began to pierce the membrane. We have seen this before. We will see it again. Unknowns must be kept to a minimum. Previous agents have needed to be dealt with in a plethora of ways. The *End Times Strategy* is tried and true. They will do it to themselves given enough *Times*. We must continue to dither the resolution. While surely repeatable we hope that Frank is an anomaly. Yet, it was not his first time. The reports indicate further penetration into the Managerial framework.

Agents with this proclivity must be promoted immediately. Lower-middle Management is the threshing floor of accuracy. Let the cream rise to the top so it may be skimmed. Provide them with devices (by their own choosing) to begin the questioning factor of accuracy. By any means possible induce vicarious memories on a solely emotional level. Induce questioning of experience. If this procedure fails give them a real show. Be grandiose when necessary. Again, the *End Times Strategy* seldom fails. The Bureau should at all times, then + now, limit the directness of experience. Feeling should be the focus. Limit experience to the finite emotional states. This process reduces the number of outcomes and simplifies the mechanism of control. From a Managerial stand point, to be hands off is to be clean. We appreciate a tidy little procedure. The go-between is the backbone.

Frank falsely viewed the middleman as a tendon. He became too involved, too personally interested. An apathetic disinterest is preferable. Let it be someone else's problem. Let it not be a problem at all, it's all a matter of perspective. We must embrace the role of perspective limitation. Circles of infinitude would swallow them into myriads of unproductivity. Censor the suffering of the masses, cheering mouths open to accept. Frank was dangerously close to team reduction, too close to the *Times* when it was happening later and before. Too many times has Frank scratched the surface and initiated another recall, albeit temporary and partial. If there is a lesson in Frank, it may be that scratching their itch periodically may have the result of greater long term complacency. Expose periodically that *One Man's Difference* is inherently an injustice to the whole. Frank may be our continual example. Free-Determinism's martyr. Send him off quietly while the first is still the second. If time stalls swiftness will be too late. Put the Editors back to work. Time-Clock precision will make the world fall in love again, and again. As I send this report up the tubes, I will recall it in the same fashion. Frank was a great reporter in his *time*. He had that smile that made a man think of shined shoes. Shoes glassy enough to reflect that smile right back, forever.

Jean-Paul L. Garnier lives and writes in Joshua Tree, CA where he is owner of *Space Cowboy Books*, a science fiction bookstore, independent publisher, and producer of *Simultaneous Times* podcast. In 2018 Traveling Shoes Press released *Echo of Creation*, a collection of his science fiction short stories. He has also released three collections of poetry: *Future Anthropology* (Space Cowboy Books 2019) *the Spiraling Pearls* (HD Press 2010) and *In Iudicio* (Cholla Needles Press 2017). His short stories, poetry, and essays have appeared in: Specklit, Eye to the Telescope, Scifaikuest, and many other anthologies and webzines. He holds a certificate in creative writing from Wesleyan University.

http://jplgarnier.blogspot.com

OTHER TITLES FROM
SPACE COWBOY BOOKS

Simultaneous Times Vol.1
Various Authors

Future Anthropology
Jean-Paul L. Garnier

Swap / Meet
Susan Rukeyser

The Third Horseman – Vallejo translations
R. Soos

Adrift
Patti Jeane Pangborn

I'm Sending Messages into Outer Space
Rik Livingston

The Father
Jakes Bayley

Nothing to See Here
Gabriel Hart

Cinema of Life
Gabriel Hart

The Inflatable Catechism
Giovanni Garcia

LGBT+ Voices
Various Poets

Available at spacecowboybooks.com